OLIVER THE LION WHO WANTS TO BE A LION

• • • •

WRITTEN BY
CYNTHIA BERCOWETZ
ILLUSTRATED BY
ERIK PFLUEGER

Barringer Publishing, Naples, Florida
www.barringerpublishing.com
Cover, graphics, layout design by Lisa Camp
Illustrations by Erik Pflueger

ISBN: 978-0-9828425-6-0

Library of Congress Cataloging-in-Publication Data
Oliver the Lion Who Wants to Be A Lion / Cynthia Bercowetz

Printed in U.S.A.

A licensed product of Lions Clubs International.

ACKNOWLEDGMENTS

● ● ● ●

I am eternally grateful to my husband for his love, his help and most of all for his encouragement in writing this book.

My husband, Herman Bercowetz, had been a Lion for 49 years. In the early stages of "Oliver the Lion Who Wants To Be A Lion" he told me he adored the name of Oliver for my cub lion. Unfortunately, he passed away before the book was finished.

I am extremely grateful to my publisher, Jeff Schlesinger, Barringer Publishing, Naples, Florida for his encouragement, assistance and help to get this book finished.

On the other hand, he told me he was grateful to learn more about the Lions all over the world and the services they do to help those in need.

My thanks to David Tetzlaff, executive director of the Naples Zoo, for his help in developing Oliver to be the brave lion he is in this book. David read my manuscript and helped me to understand Oliver as a brave and kind cub lion.

I made several trips to the zoo to see a brother and sister lion to learn about their habits. Thank you, David.

I wish to thank my illustrator Erik Pfleuger, who illustrated the wildlife and portrayed the Lions Clubs all over the world for the miraculous work they do providing eye screening and other valuable assistance to those in need.

Thanks to Robert Kyff for his attention to detail while editing the book.

My grateful thanks to Kathy Randall for her help and encouragement in writing this book. Kathy is a member of the District Cabinet of Lions in District 23B in Connecticut. She also accompanied me to Oak Brook, IL to discuss the book with the National Lions Clubs Headquarters.

I also want to thank Dan Uitti, a member of the Watertown Lions Club in Connecticut for his assistance and his knowledge of the functions of Lions Clubs.

DEDICATION FOR "OLIVER"

● ● ● ●

"Oliver the Lion" is dedicated to my late husband, Herman Bercowetz, who helped me with the research for this book. He was a Lion for more than 49 years in the Bloomfield, Connecticut Lions Club.

CHAPTER 1

● ● ● ●

Once upon a time...Wait a minute. Don't all children's stories start that way?

Anyway, this is a tale of a lion cub named Oliver who wanted to join a Lions Club. Lions Clubs are service clubs all around the world that help people who are blind or have poor vision. Lions Clubs do many other good and helpful things.

Oliver's mother and father wanted him to grow up to be a hunter. But Oliver, their smallest and cutest cub, didn't want that.

Oliver and his family lived in a lion cave atop a mountain. Oliver could look down and see the Village. He wanted to go down the mountain to walk around and see if he could find the Lions Building where many Lions met.

Oliver was a beautiful lion with a tawny, tan color. His mane was coming in very well. His eyes were piercing, yet his grimace was gentle.

CHAPTER 2

One day Oliver said to his mother and father, "I want to go down to the Village and meet the Lions and other people in the Village."

His mother and father decided against it. His mother said, "I know you want to do good and meet these Lions who do so much for those who are blind and in need of help. But you could be killed walking around the Village!"

Oliver was not happy with these thoughts. Each day, he looked down at the Village. He swished his tail; his eyes were sad.

One day, against his parents' wishes, he decided to go down to the Village.

He had never ventured down to the Square. On his way, he stopped at a brook to get a drink of cool water. A frog was bathing in the sun. Oliver asked, "Little frog, do you know the way to the Square?"

The frog said he did not know. "But," he croaked, "keep going." So Oliver continued down the mountain until he came to another brook.

There he saw a small, blonde boy trying to fish. The boy did not seem to be startled by the lion because he had never seen one before.

Oliver said, "Little boy, what is your name?"

"My name is A.J.," the boy said. "I am fishing for some fish, but they are not biting."

"Do you know how to get to the Square where I can find the Lions Club?" Oliver asked.

"I think you just keep going," A.J. said. "Are you a lion?"

"Aarrgghh," the cub growled to show A.J. he was a lion. "But I will not hurt you."

It was a beautiful day, but Oliver was tired. He thought he should rest in the shade.

When he knelt down in the grass, he saw an owl perched on a tree.

"Hello, owl," he said. "I'm looking for the Lions Building somewhere down there, but I don't know if I am going in the right direction. I am very tired."

"Whoo, whoo," the owl hooted. "That way, that way."

Oliver continued on the path until he came to a wide field.

There he saw what he thought was a scarecrow. Oliver stopped the scarecrow and asked him where the Lions Building was.

"Oh my goodness," said the scarecrow. "A real lion. I've never seen one before."

"Well, can you tell me where the Lions Building is?" Oliver asked. "I am getting very tired."

"Well, let me see," the scarecrow replied. "You could go that way." And he turned completely around. "Or you could head west," he said. "I really don't know where you can go."

As Oliver continued down the path to the Lions Building, he spotted a strange-looking man with a cowboy hat. With the man was a strange animal.

"Hello," the man said. "My name is Dan Dorfman. I am an environmentalist and work for the National Atmospheric and Oceanographic Administration. This here is my koala from Australia. We are heading back there soon. You look lost, little lion. What are you looking for?"

Oliver didn't know what the man was talking about. But he looked kind.

"I'm looking for the Lions Building," Oliver said. "Do you know where it is?"

"Well," Dan said, "I see a gold and purple building down yonder. Just keep walking, little lion. You will find it."

"Thank you," Oliver said, and continued on his journey.

He was very tired. But in front of him, further down, he saw the gold and purple building.

It was beautiful. It was getting late, so he decided to head out the following morning. He found a brook, drank its cool water and headed back to his family.

CHAPTER 3

When Oliver arrived home, his mom was very angry. She scolded him. "Why weren't you home with the rest of your family?" she asked. "I have things for you to do."

Oliver's father was not too happy either.

"You have chores to do," he said sternly.

So Oliver stood there and accepted his punishment. He also helped out his brother and sisters.

He asked if he could go out the next day to the Lions Building if he helped with the chores.

Both his parents said yes. So he did his chores.

CHAPTER 4

● ● ● ●

Oliver started on his journey the next day. By early afternoon, he was tired. He tried to take a nap by the brook.

He was very excited. After the nap, he opened his eyes and felt a warm hand on his mane.

"Hello," said a beautiful young woman dressed in white. She had a flock of sheep behind her. Her shoes were gilded.

"What's wrong?" she asked. "I am Sandy the shepherdess who lives on the other side of the mountain. I live with my mom and two beautiful dogs, Buckeye and Bella."

Oliver said he could not find the Lions Building.

"Come, I will show you," Sandy smiled.

Then she proceeded to walk down the mountain, and the flock of sheep followed her.

As she walked, she sang:

"My name is Sandy Slane; I have a flock of sheep.

Their fleece is white as snow.

And everywhere I go, my sheep are sure to go."

What a sight they were! Oliver slowly followed Sandy the shepherdess and the flock of sheep as they descended the mountain.

At the bottom of the mountain, Sandy pointed out the gold and purple building.

She smiled, "There you are, you beautiful lion."

She waved, and Oliver walked toward the building.

Just moments before Oliver entered the building, Dr. Robert Maximillan Friedler, a retired kidney specialist, walked into the Lions Building.

He introduced himself to the Lions who were testing people's eyes.

Dr. Friedler had grown up in Chile. He had many skills as a doctor.

"Hello," he said. "I'm Dr. Friedler. I have skills to help you with the wonderful work that you do here."

Normand Messier, a Past District Governor representing his club from Windsor Locks, Connecticut, shook his hand warmly.

District Governor is a high achievement for a Lion. He or she has been a president of their club, attended many club meetings and is an exemplary Lion.

"We need all the help we can get!" he said.

Oliver was just about to walk into the building.

Many Lions looked out and saw Sandy the shepherdess leaving with her flock. They gasped.

Oliver saw many men and women around the building. Everyone looked so funny to him. Almost everyone had a yellow vest on.

He said to one Lion, "May I go into your building?"

The Lion jumped two feet when he saw the lion.

He ran into the building to tell the other Lions.

"Let him come in," said Lion Howard Freedman, a very friendly Lion from the Naples Lions Club in Florida.

So Oliver was welcomed in.

Oliver lay down right in the middle of the Lions Building. He was very tired.

"Oh my!" said Lion Howie kindly. "What do you want?"

Oliver replied, "I want to know what Lions do."

So Lion Howie said, "We're doing an eye screening today. These people here have come to get many tests – eyes, blood pressure, diabetes testing – and many other services offered by Lions, nurses and eye specialists."

"Please," Oliver begged. "I would like to see an eye screening."

A young, attractive Lion said, "We also have a booth for low vision."

"WOW!" Oliver said. "I would like to watch!"

Everyone saw that Oliver was a friendly lion, and they came over to greet him. He was such a happy lion cub.

CHAPTER 5

● ● ● ●

Oliver went over to another booth.

"Hello," said Len Johnson, another Past District Governor from Connecticut. "This is a booth named for Helen Keller."

"Who is she?" Oliver asked.

"Well, she was a great lady," Lion Len explained. "She couldn't speak or hear or see when she was very small, but her teacher Anne Sullivan taught her sign language and how to speak. Helen became a famous advocate for handicapped people and inspired Lions all over the world to give them the spirit to accomplish what they have done for many years."

HELEN KELLER
(1880-1968)

CHAPTER 6

● ● ● ●

Oliver saw a lovely woman in a Lions uniform standing behind some devices to help people see better.

He approached her.

Some of the Lions were afraid of this cub lion who had come into their building.

But this Lion spoke softly to Oliver.

"Can I help you?" she asked.

Oliver liked her right away. "Hello," he said. "My name is Oliver. I live in the mountains. What are you doing?"

"My name is Carolyn Messier," she said. "I help anyone with low vision."

Oliver looked at her and asked what she meant. He looked dumbfounded.

"You mean some people cannot see?" he asked.

"Yes," Carolyn said. "At our Low Vision Center in Connecticut most of our people cannot see well."

She explained that there are many devices to aid them. "In the United States," she said, "someone becomes blind or visually impaired every seven minutes."

"My goodness!" Oliver said.

As Oliver roamed around the building, he saw many Lions helping people.

He asked a tall, friendly-looking man who was examining a young boy, "What are you doing?"

"We are ophthalmologists* who are screening the eyes of children to see if they have vision defects," he replied.

Oliver remembered now that he had met this friendly Lion when he first came in. He said his name was Dr. Howie Freedman.

"Oh," said Oliver. "Can you test MY eyes?"

"No," Dr. Freedman said. "We test humans only, but thanks for asking."

But he told Oliver that the Naples Zoo in Florida or any zoo has excellent vets who do these procedures on animals. (*An ophthalmologist is an eye specialist.)

CHAPTER 7

● ○ ● ○

"Well, how do lions and other animals get tested?" Oliver thought as he sat down on his tail.

A Lion called out to him, "C'mon over here." Oliver went and asked his name.

"My name is Bob Woomer," he said. "What are you doing here, buddy?" he asked Oliver. "We don't mind, but we've never had a visit from the animal kingdom before."

Oliver wagged his bushy tail. "I like the Lions," he said. "Can I be a Lion?"

Bob shook his head sadly and said, "I'm afraid not. You're a lion."

"But you are a Lion, and you help people," Oliver stammered.

Lion Bob explained to Oliver that you have to be human to be a Lion. He sadly wished that others were as dedicated as this lion was.

Oliver was sad. He wanted to help people, but he knew he couldn't join the Lions Club.

"Come back again," Lion Bob said. "You're always welcome here."

Oliver swished his bushy tail and walked slowly, very slowly, toward his home.

CHAPTER 8

One early evening, Oliver was returning to his home atop the mountaintop.

He was very, very tired. He felt he must rest for a day or two.

In the far corner of his eye, he saw flames coming from a barn. He recognized it as Old McCaffery's barn.

The flames grew higher and higher. "What should I do?" the concerned lion thought.

He went to the barn and saw that the man inside was in danger.

The fire was so hot that it singed some of Oliver's mane. What should he do?

As the flames burned down the barn, he ran to the fire department. The firefighters saw a lion running toward them.

"Fire! Fire!" Oliver roared.

They ran with him to the barn. Old McCaffery had collapsed, but the firefighters were able to rescue him because he was near the door.

The man was placed in an ambulance, which headed to the nearest hospital.

Oliver, who had been overcome by smoke, was taken to the emergency clinic of a veterinary hospital.

There was so much commotion. Oliver recuperated at the hospital, but he was very weak.

Old McCaffery recovered in a few days, and luckily he was all right. His family said he would never smoke again. A lit cigarette had started the flames.

But fortunately both Old McCaffery and Oliver survived this harrowing experience.

CHAPTER 9

● ● ● ●

Oliver's mom and dad were proud of him. They sat in the veterinary hospital and were so proud of all the attention that Oliver was receiving. The town newspaper, the mayor and many of the Lions from the Lions Building assembled in the Town Square.

"Oh, what a beautiful day," Oliver thought. If only he had felt better.

He looked up at everyone and said, "Thank you for coming." They all cheered.

Several weeks later, the mayor issued a proclamation in the Town Square. Everyone came. Oliver and his family were there.

TOWN OF JUSTICE

PROCLAMATION

WHEREAS, Oliver the lion lives with his parents in the mountains; and

WHEREAS, Oliver is a brave lion; and

WHEREAS, Oliver notifies the fire department that Mr. McCaffery's barn is burning; and

WHEREAS, Oliver gets singed by the fire trying to help blind Mr. McCaffery, and is taken to the veterinarian hospital for treatment; and

WHEREAS, Oliver is visited by Lions doing an eye screening at the Lions Building, and

WHEREAS, Mr. McCaffery and Oliver are all right, and

NOW, THEREFORE, I, Melody A. Currey, Mayor of the Town, do hereby proclaim

Oliver the Lion is the Bravest Lion we know!

From Lions Everywhere

IN WITNESS THEREOF, I herewith set my hand

Melody A. Currey, Mayor

CHAPTER 10

● ● ● ●

When Oliver felt better, he went to visit Old McCaffery at the hospital. Old McCaffery was coming along well, but he had to stay in the hospital for an undisclosed amount of time.

He was happy to see Oliver. So was his family. They said that he would NEVER smoke in the barn again.

When everyone was better, a special meeting was held at the Lions Building. It was decided that Oliver could be installed as a mascot for the Lions Club, the Good Samaritan Lions Club.

"What is a Good Samaritan Club?" Oliver asked.

He was told that it meant that the club would perform good deeds for the community.

Past District Governor Bob Woomer of the Naples Nites of Naples, Florida, would perform the installation, together with Past District Governor Syd Schulman of the Lions Club in Bloomfield, Connecticut. They also would introduce Oliver to members of the club. No officers were selected.

"Oliver, please step forward," they said in unison.

Oliver did.

Bob Woomer said, "The Lions are the largest service-oriented group of clubs under an international organization. Each member enjoys fellowship, develops leadership and dedicates part of his or her time to helping those in need in their own community first, but also in the rest of the world.

"The member we are inducting tonight as a mascot has been invited to join the over 1.3 million Lions in 206 countries and geographical areas around the world who support the Lions Motto: 'We Serve.'

"At this time, I would like Past District Governor Syd Schulman to come forward again."

Syd Schulman lit a purple candle.

He explained that the colors of purple and gold were selected as the official colors of the Lions Club in 1917. To Lions, purple represents loyalty to country, friends, to one's self and to integrity of mind and heart. It is the color of strength, courage and dedication to a cause.

Syd addressed Oliver and said, "Gold symbolizes sincerity of purpose and liberality in judgment, as you displayed, Oliver, in saving Mr. McCaffery and notifying the fire department.

"We use the white candle to symbolize the International Association of Lions Clubs because white represents truth.

"Since you have expressed a desire to affiliate with this Club and with Lions Clubs International, I will now ask that you give us the Lions' Roar."

Oliver stood on his hind feet and gave a loud roar. His parents joined in.

Lion Syd placed an emblem with gold letters around Oliver's neck. It had lion profiles on either side, facing away from the center.

Lion Bob said that, symbolically, the lions are facing both past and future, proud of their past and confident of their future.

Cub Lion Oliver was so proud. He turned around to show the emblem to his parents and the rest of the family.

Lion Syd said to the members of the Lions, "Will you fulfill the following obligations to the new mascot?

"Make Oliver feel welcome by introducing him to all of our Club members?

"Provide him with information about your clubs, their officers and the Lions constitution?

"Be ready to answer any questions he might have on the operation of the Lions Club? Assist him in developing into an outstanding Lion?"

The Lions responded loudly, "WE WILL!"

Bob Woomer finished the ceremony for Oliver. He said, "Oliver, wear your emblem constantly with pride.

"Let me congratulate you and welcome you into the greatest of all service organizations: the International Association of Lions Clubs. We are all proud and happy to have you as the mascot of the Good Samaritan Lions Club."

What a beautiful day it was. The sun was shining, and it looked as if it were shining on Oliver's emblem. Everyone applauded, even some of the monkeys who came to visit from their habitats.

THE END

EPILOGUE

● ● ● ●

Oliver is not a real lion, but I am sure he will capture the hearts of everyone.

I am a Lion, and I am very proud to be one. I am a Lion in the Bloomfield, Connecticut, Lions Club as a full member. In Naples, Florida, I am a member of the Lions Club as an associate member.

LIONS CODE OF ETHICS

TO SHOW my faith in the worthiness of my vocations by industrious application to the end that I may merit a reputation for quality of service.

TO SEEK success and to demand all fair remuneration or profit as my just due, but to accept no profit or success at the price of my own self-respect lost because of unfair advantage taken or because of questionable acts on my part.

TO REMEMBER that in building up my business it is not necessary to tear down another's, to be loyal to my clients or customers and true to myself.

WHENEVER a doubt arises as to the right or ethics of my position or action toward others, to resolve such doubt against myself.

TO HOLD friendship as an end and not a means. To hold that true friendship exists not on account of the service performed by one to another, but that true friendship demands nothing but accepts service in the spirit in which it is given.

ALWAYS to bear in mind my obligation as a citizen to my nation, my state and my community and to give them my unswerving loyalty in word, act and deed. To give them freely of my time, labor and means.

TO AID others by giving my sympathy to those in distress, my aid to the weak, and my substance to the needy.

TO BE CAREFUL with my criticism and liberal with my praise; to build up and not destroy.